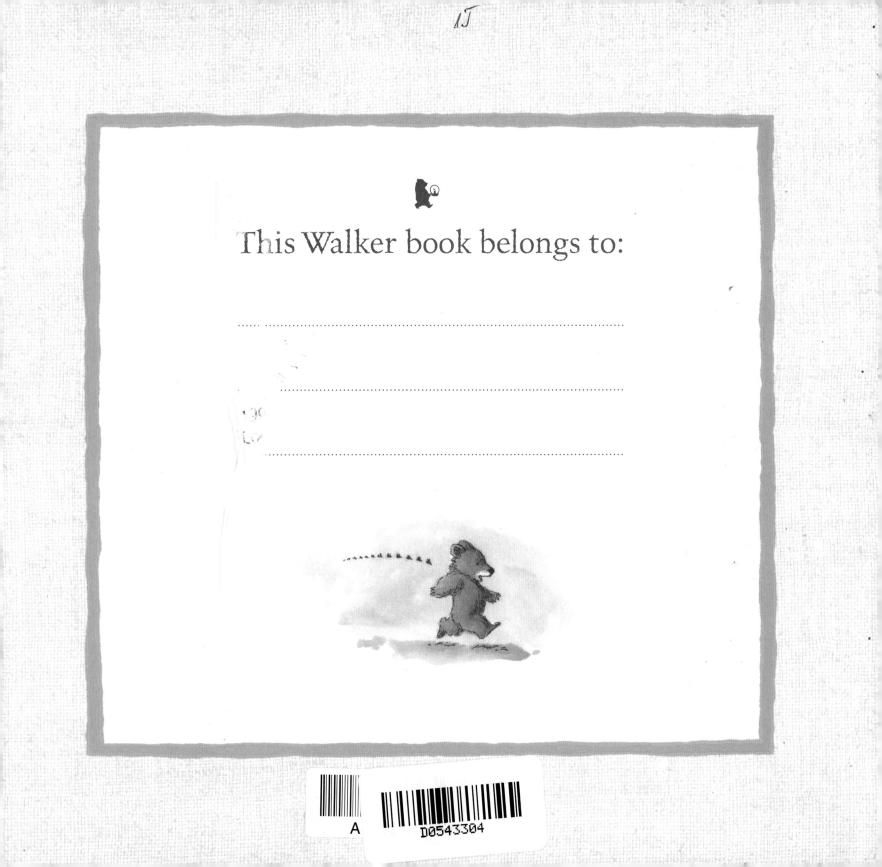

This Walker book belongs to:

....

....

....

For Popsy

A. L. and D. M.

First published 2011 by Walker Books Ltd
87 Vauxhall Walk, London SE11 5HJ

This edition published 2012

2 4 6 8 10 9 7 5 3 1

Text © 2011 Albert Lamb
Illustrations © 2011 David McPhail

The right of Albert Lamb and David McPhail to be identified as
author and illustrator respectively of this work has been asserted by them
in accordance with the Copyright, Designs and Patents Act 1988

This book has been typeset in Quercus

Printed in China

British Library Cataloguing in Publication Data:
a catalogue record for this book is available from the British Library

ISBN 978-1-4063-3775-4

www.walker.co.uk

Tell Me the Day Backwards

Albert Lamb   illustrated by David McPhail

WALKER BOOKS
AND SUBSIDIARIES
LONDON • BOSTON • SYDNEY • AUCKLAND

"Let's play that game we used to play last summer," said Timmy Bear as he got into bed for the night. "Let's play Tell Me the Day Backwards."

"Oh, I remember that game," Mummy Bear said as she tucked him in. "You start."

"Tonight, before I got into bed, I brushed my teeth in the stream."

"Yes, that's right," said Mummy Bear. "That was after we watched the sunset from the top of the hill. And do you remember what happened before that?"

"I remember! Daddy Bear brought us a yummy picnic, and we ate supper together."

"And what happened before that?"

"Before that, I lay on top of the big rock, sunning myself. It made my fur get toasty!"

"And before that?"

"Daddy Bear had to pull me out of the deep pool in the river."

"Yes, that was terrible," said Mummy Bear.

"And before that, I was looking at a big scary fish face under the water," said Timmy Bear. "That was terrible, too."

"It must have been," said Mummy Bear. "What happened before that?"

"I ran and jumped off the high, high rock into the deep pool."

"And before that?"

"I was chased by bees, and they were stinging me! I couldn't run fast enough to get away from them."

"And before that?"

"Before that, I was eating some of the most delicious honey in the whole world!"

"And before that?"

"Before that, I discovered an old rotten tree stump with a dusty old beehive hidden inside it."

"And that's when you should have come and found me!" Mummy Bear reminded Timmy.

"Yes, Mummy. And before that, I was creeping through the undergrowth, just like a crafty fox. But I don't remember anything before that."

"I remember!" said Mummy Bear. "Before that, you and I ate a breakfast of lovely ants at the anthill."

"That was yummy, too!" said Timmy Bear.

"And what happened before that?"

"Before that was early. The sun was just coming up, and you and I stepped out of the cave. We saw all those purple butterflies!"

"And before that?"

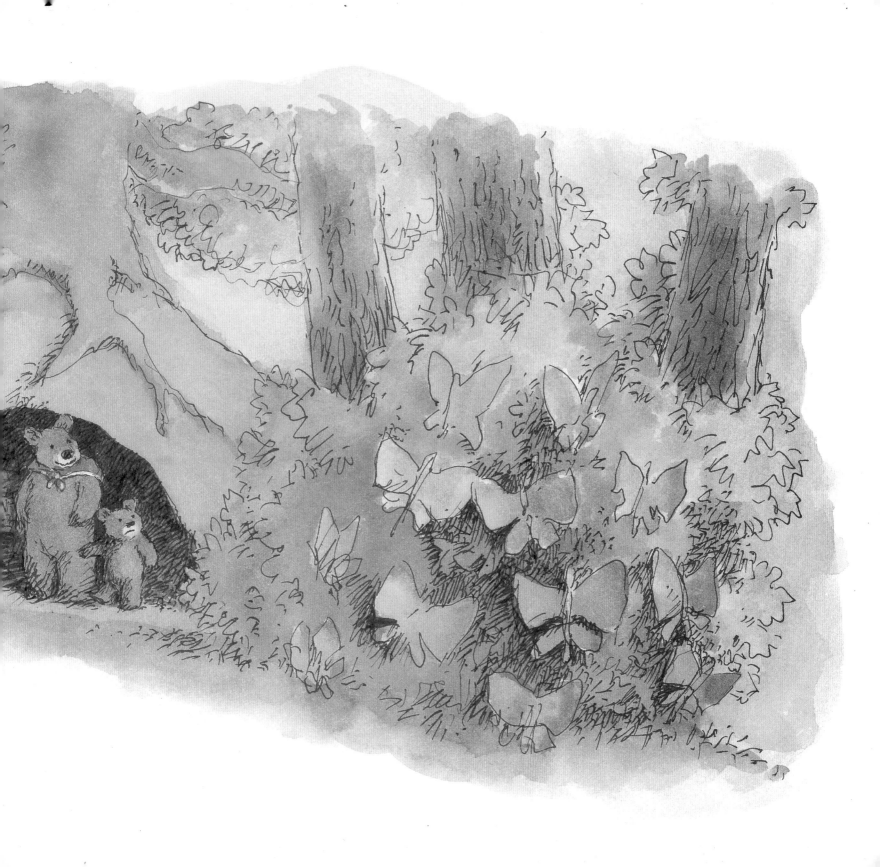

"Before that, I think you were sitting by my bed, waking me up."

"Yes," said Mummy Bear. "And can you remember the important thing that happened right before that?"

"Before this morning, I slept and slept and slept; you and me and Daddy Bear, we slept a deep sleep all through the whole long, cold winter."

"That's right," said Mummy Bear. "But tonight we'll sleep for just one night."

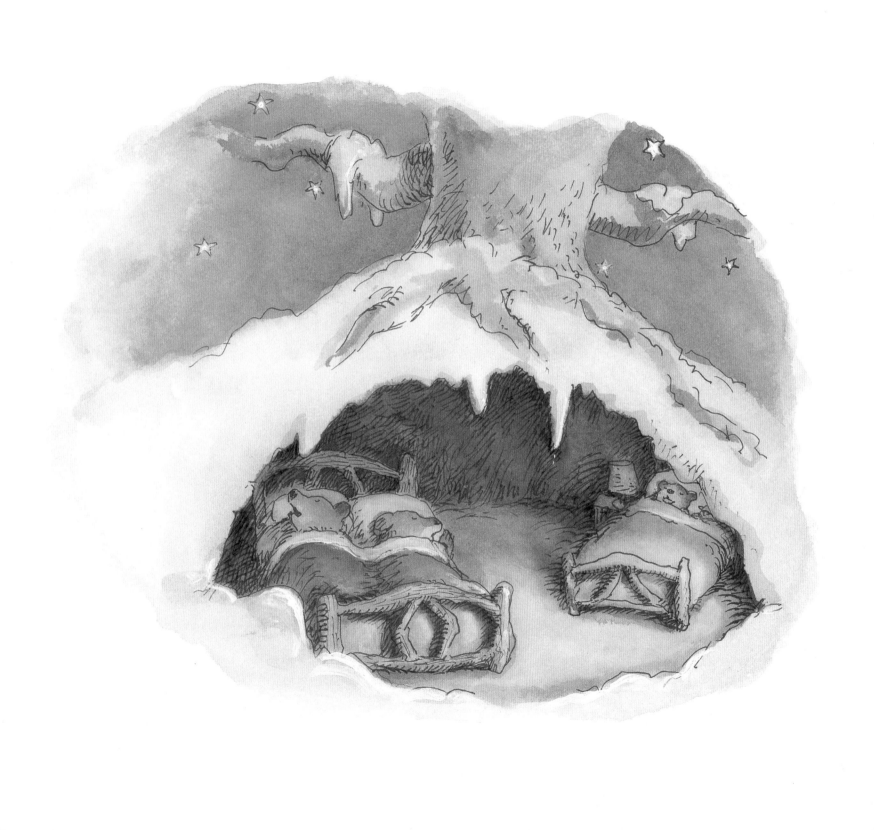

Timmy Bear was very sleepy now.

"Good night, Mummy Bear."

"Good night, Timmy. Sleep tight."

Timmy Bear closed his eyes, and soon he was fast asleep.

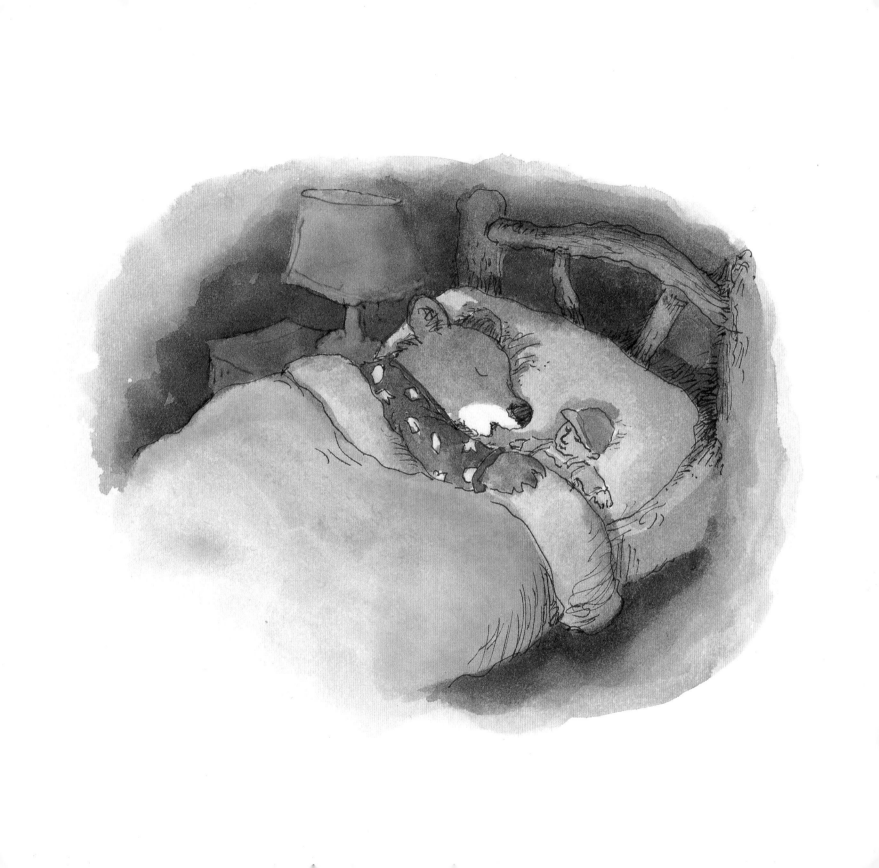

Albert Lamb has worked as a cartoonist, a musician and a writer. About this book, he says, "My wife used to play this game with her kids when they were little. She gave me the title, but the bears are all mine." Albert Lamb was born in the USA in Boston, Massachusetts, but now lives in the UK in the Cotswolds.

David McPhail has been an artist ever since childhood. He has written and illustrated more than fifty books for children. About this book, he says, "When I first read this story I thought that it was written especially for me. It has irresistible charm – how could I not want to draw pictures for it?" David McPhail lives in the USA in New Hampshire.